HENRIETTA

David Mamet

Illustrated by Elizabeth Dahlie

Houghton Mifflin Company   Boston New York 1999

2

*O*nce there was a Pig, and you may remark there was a pig more than once, and all of it is true.

This pig, I say, however, lived on an Eastern Isle, and walked its beaches one year to the next, engrossed in thought and study.

Then to Boston, Athens of the North, did our pig go—for Boston sets itself up as our Seat of Learning, and have not the Luminaries in all the fields issued from there these last three hundred years?

*T*his pig aspired
to the Law.

From earliest youth,
she saw herself lay down the
yellow tablet and address the
jury with that mix of common
sense and erudition so dear to
our Country's heart.

And having seen the barriers
to the Professions crumble
before now this and now that
disadvantaged group, she presented
herself at the institution of her choice.

The institution, however, could neither admit nor acknowledge her, as she had no credentials save an honest and inquiring mind, the tests for which take time. And the school had no time for Henrietta.

9

8

One season passed into the next, and she haunted the libraries and folded herself into the backs of the lecture halls, until she'd been discovered one too many times and then ejected and barred as a nuisance.

She watched the river,

12

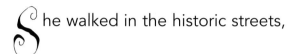She walked in the historic streets,

She slept underneath a bridge,

16

And as her resources diminished, she wondered what she might have done to have come to another end.

And she despaired, until that day the absence of which would deservedly decrease your admiration of this book, that day when she saw the Old Vagabond rise, once again, from his bench, and cast about for his glasses. The day was drawing in and it was cold, and she saw the Old Man was anxious and she joined him in his search, and when it proved bootless, she asked if she might see him home.

"For this relief, much thanks," he said, and she responded, "*Hamlet*, Act One, Scene One." "Well remembered, boy," he said, so shortsighted was he. She smiled and took his arm.

"Four legs at morning, two at noon, and three at the close of day," he said.

"*Oedipus*," she responded.

"Well remembered and well read," said the Old Man, who, it will surprise no one, was the President of this Great University. "Tell me, boy, where did you get your education?"

"Education," she responded, "is most often useless, save in those cases it is near superfluous."

"Fielding, *Jonathan Wild,*" he said, and so they continued, till they were settled by the fire in his book-lined home.

23

24

He fitted his spare spectacles to his nose, and fixed his gaze on the visitor, while Henrietta waited for the effect her identity might have on him.

"You've been of service to me, miss," he said. "Now, how may I reciprocate?"

26

"Sir," she said, "you see before you one who, like our Sainted Lincoln, burns to serve through the medium of the Law . . ."

So she began her speech, and so she continued through her enrollment, her student career, and till, it will not surprise you, she stood on the dais to give the Commencement Address.

"Let us not be sentimental," she said, "over the accomplishments of one who comes from a disadvantaged group, but let us work for social justice."

$\mathcal{A}$nd she went on to speak of the need for justice, and she worked for it, and her work took her to that high place she enjoys today.

$\mathcal{A}$nd her accomplishments, of course, have been claimed by the School and the City, but she continues to credit her family, her friends, her books, and her island.

For information about permission
to reproduce selections from this book, write to
Permissions, Houghton Mifflin Company,
215 Park Avenue South, New York, New York 10003.

Book design by Lisa Diercks
Typeset in Avenir (Adobe)
and Housemaid (House Industries)

Library of Congress Cataloging-in-Publication Data
is available.

ISBN 0-618-00416-5

Printed in the United States of America

WOZ 10 9 8 7 6 5 4 3 2 1